The
Mucker's Tale

Also by Joan Lennon and published by
Catnip in our Tales from the Keep series:

The Ferret Princess
Wag and the King

For older readers:

A Slightly Jones Mystery The Case of the
London Dragonfish

Tales *from the* Keep

The Mucker's Tale

Joan Lennon   Scoular Anderson

To everyone who ever wishes they had
a flying horse of their own

CATNIP BOOKS
Published by Catnip Publishing Ltd
14 Greville Street
London EC1N 8SB

First published 2010
1 3 5 7 9 10 8 6 4 2

Text copyright © Joan Lennon 2010
Illustrations copyright © Scoular Anderson 2010
The moral rights of the author and illustrator have been asserted

A CIP catalogue record for this book is available from the
British Library

ISBN 978-1-846470-93-6

Printed in Poland

www.catnippublishing.co.uk

Contents

Chapter One

The Wizard and the Sweeper Boy

The ragged boy leaned on his broom
and sighed as the wizard walked past.
Once again, he hadn't had the nerve

to speak to the old man, to ask him the questions that filled his mind day and night …

KABOOM!

The wizard had just started up the steps to his magnificent house when the street shook and a cloud of smelly purple smoke billowed out of the front door. He turned around quickly and went back down again.

He noticed that a ragged boy with a broom was watching him, and he smiled.

"I think I'll just sit out on the steps for a bit, and let that settle," the wizard said to him. "Perhaps you'd like to join me?"

The ragged boy's eyes went very big, but he came over anyway and sat down beside the wizard.

"What's your name?" the old man

asked. He was wearing a fabulously pointy hat and fancy robes and had a spectacularly long white beard, but he had a kind voice.

"They call me Sweeper, Honoured Sir," the boy said. "Because that's my job. I sweep the streets."

The old man chuckled. "You know what they used to call me when I was your age?" he said. "Mucker!"

The boy couldn't believe it. "You mean – you weren't always a wizard?" he exclaimed.

"Oh no – not by a long shot! Once I was just a stable boy, and nobody called me 'Honoured Sir'! No, like I said, everybody called me 'Mucker'!"

And the wizard's mind went back to those long ago days and, as Sweeper listened, he began to tell a story …

Chapter Two

Kingdom in the Sky

"Hey, Mucker!"

Oh yes, that was me. I grew up in a tiny kingdom, hidden so high in the mountains that the clouds kept bumping into the castle walls. From as soon as I was tall enough to handle a broom, I'd been the stable boy.

The castle stable wasn't very big, but it still needed a lot of sweeping because, as you know, all horses are really, really good at producing manure. And once it's been produced, somebody has to muck it all out, and that somebody was me.

I didn't mind. Not too much, anyway. Because the horses I was sweeping up after weren't just *ordinary* horses. Not by a long shot. *Our* horses could *fly*.

You don't see flying horses much outside the mountains. They are creatures of the cold, feeding on meadow grass and pine trees and thriving in the frigid air. Also, although they *can* take off from a flat running start, they much prefer a decent launching cliff to get airborne, and they are at their best with the kind of savage winds that batter round mountain peaks like ours.

You might say I was really lucky, getting to work with such fabulous animals. And I was! But the problem was, there was something I wanted to do even more.

I wanted to be a wizard.

And I wasn't the only one.

Even though our kingdom was small and out of the way, it still had everything a kingdom *should* have. We had an extremely honourable King (who was, sadly, a widower), a collection of Courtiers, some Faithful Old Retainers, the bravest of brave Guardsmen, a deliciously talented Cook, a Court Wizard (whose name

was Magnus the Magnificent) ... and a princess. Her name was Emmeline.

You might say *she* was really lucky, too, being a princess. But there was something she wanted to be doing, even more than princessing, just like me. She wanted to be a wizard too.

We used to meet up in the stables and complain about our lives. (Emmeline was as good with the flying horses as I was. She would

practise her singing on them and brush
the gunk out of their tails and lend a hand
when my two just weren't enough. She
was also teaching me to read, as I had no
time for proper schooling.)

"My father makes me take singing
lessons and history lessons and algebra
lessons, but he won't let me take lessons

from Magnus the Magnificent," moaned Emmeline. "He says princesses don't need to know how to do magic."

"Same here," I moaned back. "Stable boys don't need to know how to do magic either."

"I don't think he'll ever change his mind," sighed Emmeline. "*Nothing* ever changes around here."

"Nothing ever changes, and nothing ever happens," I sighed back.

And it really did feel like that. It felt as if everything would stay just the way it was for at least a hundred million years. Until, one day, something *did* happen, and *everything* changed.

That was the day the raiders came …

Chapter Three

The Day the Raiders Came

It wasn't as if we didn't have walls and gates and the bravest of Guardsmen. We did. But not even the oldest Old Retainer could remember a time when anyone had tried to *attack* us. Being small and remote, pretty much on the top of the world, had kept us safe and unnoticed for, well, forever. But all that was about to change.

The rotten raiders got into the castle by pretending to be a travelling merchant and his servants. Goodness knows what the Guardsmen thought they'd be selling, so far off the beaten

track. Whatever it was, the gates were opened and in they came, as easy as anything. Then, the moment they were safely inside our walls, they pulled out more daggers and swords than we had in out entire armoury – *and they grabbed Princess Emmeline!*

"Get everyone into the Throne Room NOW!" snarled the leader, a scrawny, straw-haired man with pale, mean eyes. "And if you value this little missy, you won't take all day about it, either!"

Word spread like fire and soon every soul in the castle had gathered in the Throne Room, from the oldest Retainer to the King himself. I could barely get in through the door, the room was so packed, but I managed to climb up on a chest to see over everybody's heads. And there was Emmeline, with one of the henchmen gripping her roughly by the arm, her face pale but her back straight.

The King turned to the leader.

"May we know the name of the man who is treating a princess with so little respect?" he said in a deep voice.

"You don't *know* who I am?" The

leader of the ruffians seemed astonished, and his henchmen pulled shocked faces. "Well, what can you expect from a bunch of hill-fools? Allow me to educate you. I am Prince Franck."

"Indeed?" said the King, making it clear that he was not much impressed by this. "And what is it you want with my daughter?"

Prince Franck laughed, but he turned an angry red too.

"What, this little no-nothing two-a-penny mountain princess? I don't want her at all, except as a hostage!" he sneered. He began to strut up and down as he talked.

I couldn't help noticing how skinny his legs were. He looked a lot like a chicken parading around like that, but somehow it didn't seem very funny just then.

"No, I'm here for something much more valuable. Something that is going to change the future of a *proper* kingdom – *mine!*"

The King said, "Didn't you say you were only a prince?"

"A prince – for *now*. My father is an old man. He won't last much longer."

"Hasn't he chosen his heir?"

"Oh, he's chosen all right." Franck's voice was venomous. "He's chosen my brother to get everything after his death."

"So that is that, surely." The King was an honourable man. You could see he really didn't understand anyone like the Prince at all.

"Yeah, right," Franck sneered, and his men snorted and made rude faces.

What does he want? I thought. I couldn't believe this was really happening. *If he doesn't want Emmeline, what's he after?*

Then Prince Franck spoke again and

it all became horribly clear.

"I'm here to take your flying horses," he announced. "I'm going to take them, every last one, and I'm going to fly them over my brother's castles and

drop boulders until everyone's dead or
they make *me* the king. Oh, and unless
you, and every man and woman you're
the king of, vows not to do one single,
solitary thing to stop me, I'll kill your
daughter."

Chapter Four

The Vile Prince Franck

There was a horrified gasp, and then silence. There could be no arguing with this ghastly excuse for a prince.

"Good. Very sensible," Franck sneered. "Now, I can't be bothered taking an oath off this lot one at a time." And he waved a dismissive hand at us all. Then he turned to our King. "But if *you* take the vow for everybody, they'll have to obey you. That's how it works with us royalty, doesn't it." And he smirked and squirmed in a way that obviously made our King want to go away and have a bath.

Nevertheless he said, "Give me back my daughter, and you have my word, that no man I am king of will try to stop you."

"*Or* woman!" Franck cried. "You'll not catch me out with that old trap! Say it straight, and no tricks."

Our King, who would never have considered anything tricksy or underhanded in a hundred years, gave him a look of deep scorn, but repeated the oath again anyway.

"No man or woman that I am king of will try to stop you. You have my word. Give me back my daughter."

Prince Franck stared round the room, a big stupid grin of triumph on his face, and then flicked a finger at the thug holding the Princess.

"Let her go. We don't need *her* any more!"

The henchman laughed and gave Princess Emmeline a shove forward. She staggered, but didn't fall. For a moment I thought our King was going to punch the man in the face, but with an effort he restrained himself. He wasn't supposed to do things like that, being royal. He probably wanted to give his daughter a big hug too, but he didn't.

"Go to your room now, my dear," he said to her instead, gentle but firm, and with her back still as straight as a tree, the Princess went.

I slipped out of the room after her.

"Princess?"

She turned on me so fast I had to jump back. Her face was furious. "He sent me to my room! Like a useless child! Our beautiful horses are going to be stolen away and all I'm good for is to be a hostage – and then get sent to my room! Well, I won't have it. We're going to *stop* those thieving knaves."

I was shocked. "But we *can't*!" I said. "Your father agreed, on his honour, that no man or woman in the kingdom would lift a finger to stop them."

"That's right," snapped Emmeline. "And we're neither. We're children. Come on!"

We ran as fast as we could, by the back ways right up to the top of the main tower, the one that looks down into the courtyard. The stables opened off from that courtyard, so it was the best place to get an idea of what was going on. It was a long climb, and we were both out of breath by the time we got there.

"We should be able to see what's happening," I whispered to the Princess, "but we must be careful that they don't see *us*."

She nodded, and together we crept to the parapet and peered over.

I don't know what I thought I was going to see – it could hardly have been anything good! – but I was totally unprepared for the scene that lay below.

The sound of shouts and cursing was loud and painfully clear. The courtyard was full of great wooden cages on wheels, with teams of oxen yoked to them. The raiders must have left them

just out of sight down the road, but now they'd been dragged up, and they were loading our flying horses into them. But the cowards were taking no chances.

It hurt like a punch in the stomach to see our horses like that, blindfolded and haltered and with their beautiful wings tied to their sides with ropes. They had never known even an unkind word – how could they understand being treated like this? The thought of them dragged away to the hot flatlands in the hands of men like Franck made me want to race down and, and … and what?

I didn't realise I'd started shaking until the Princess put her hand on my arm and drew me back from the edge.

"Thank goodness the colts are out in the far meadow," she said. "That's at least something. Now, we need to think … what are we going to do?"

I stared at her, feeling absolutely desperate. All I could think about was how there wasn't a man or woman in the entire kingdom who could stop the horrible Prince and his wretched raiders from stealing those horses. There was only *us* – and at that moment I couldn't see what we could *possibly* do.

But Emmeline had no doubts.

"Come on, Mucker – don't you see? It's just like in the stories," she whispered, her eyes shining. "When it looks as if

all is lost, and anyone who *could* save the day *can't*, and there's only the most unlikely people left, and they discover that they have *the one special thing* that's the only *possible* way to beat the baddies."

I tried to interrupt, but she was still talking.

"The most unlikely people – that would definitely be us. And the one special thing … but what would *that* be? Think, Emmeline, think! All those princessing lessons I've had – all that singing and history and algebra – oh, why didn't I learn anything *useful*?! Never mind, it'll come to us, I know it will. We'll think on the way. Let's go!"

She was already up and starting for the stairs, but I called her back.

"Princess! No! Wait!"

She paused. "What is it? There's no
time to lose — come *on*!"

I shook my head. "No, not yet.
We can't go after them yet — we'd be
spotted right away. There's no cover for
the first part of that road. We need to let
them get ahead, wait till they stop for
the night …"

With a big sigh, she came back.
"You're right, I guess. But I hate like
anything letting them just *go*!"

"I know. I hate it too." But my mind

wasn't completely
on her just at that
moment. "It's
a good thing
we're both
titchy," I muttered.

She stiffened. "What did you just call me?!"

"I called you titchy. Which is a good thing. A grown person would be too heavy for the colts." *Maybe it was a bad idea ...*

Then her eyes went wide. "We're going to follow on the colts! You're a genius! It's the perfect way to catch up with the raiders."

"We still don't know what we'll do when we get there," I said.

But I could tell she wasn't listening to me any more.

"I'll meet you back here in a bit," she said. "There's something I've got to get …"

Chapter Five

The One Special Thing

The raiders were long gone by the time the Princess returned. She was out of breath and clutching a heavy bundle in her arms.

"What…?" I asked but she'd already started to unpack.

"Jackets." (Nobody flies in the mountains wearing just indoor clothes.) "Gloves. Some food. And … the one special thing!"

She had a big triumphant grin all over her face.

"What is it?" I asked.

"Magnus the Magnificent's spell

book!" she
crowed.

"But … but …
you *stole* it?!" I stammered.

She shrugged. "Just borrowed. We'll
give it back afterwards."

I looked at the book doubtfully. It
was big and impressive and black, with
stars on the cover and complicated
looking writing on the inside.

"You know … I can't read very well
yet …" I muttered.

"But I can!" cried Emmeline.
"Ready? Let's go!"

The castle was as stirred up as an
anthill, with people rushing around

and whispering in shocked little groups and then rushing around some more. We were almost noticed a dozen times over, but at last we made it to the back gate and panted up the mountainside towards the far meadow.

The colts weren't ready for saddles yet, or bridles either. I was worried it would take for ever to catch any – they could be very skittish and tended to treat everything as a game of tag. But I needn't have worried. As soon as the colts heard us coming, they just trotted up, and Princess Emmeline was immediately surrounded by soft noses and feathery wings.

"Which two shall we take?" she asked.

"Hiho for me," I said, pointing. "And Piddler for you. They're the strongest. I

only hope the rest won't decide to come as well – they never want to miss out on anything."

The Princess was already on Piddler's back. She settled herself between his wings as the colt pranced about, and called to me, "Hurry up! It's time we were off."

She'd urged her steed into a run and was heading for the launching cliff

before I'd even put a hand on Hiho. I
scrambled up and we raced after her –
trailing the rest of the herd who, as I'd
feared, had no intention of being left
out of whatever adventure was on offer.
As Hiho reached the edge and dropped
off into the sky, there was Emmeline
on Piddler, catching the up draught,
swooping away, laughing in excitement.

The colts didn't care where we were
going – they were having too much fun.
The sun was beginning to set behind
the mountains as we reached the place
where the road entered the forest. There
was a clearing not too far along that,
if I'd guessed right, the raiders would
use to overnight in, so I headed for
the other side of the trees. There was a
place there that had a spring and good
pasture for the colts and enough height

so we could use it to launch from when they needed to take off again.

The moment we landed, the colts wasted no time beginning to graze, and Emmeline and I headed off stealthily into the forest.

"Remember, I don't exactly know what I'm doing," she whispered to me. "We need to get really close if my magic's going to work."

"As close as we can, without being spotted," I said.

It was getting dark under the trees, but I saw her nod. Then she grabbed my arm and pointed. A light was flickering up ahead. It was a cooking fire. We had found the raiders' camp.

Franck and his

men *had* decided to spend the night
in the clearing. As we crept closer, we
could see them moving about, making
dinner, squabbling about who got to
sit on which log. Prince Franck was
complaining loudly about not having a
proper feather bed to sleep in.

There was no sign of the oxen. They
must have pastured them away from
their camp. (We were lucky not to
have stumbled upon them – oxen are
noisy creatures when startled.) The
raiders had kept their stolen property
in plain view, though. The cages with
the flying horses were parked over to
one side of the clearing. The horses had
been packed in so tightly that there
wasn't room for them to lie down, and
I could hear the occasional sound as
they shifted slightly, trying to find some

comfort. I could feel myself starting to
shake with anger again, but I pushed it
aside. It wasn't time for that.

It was time for Emmeline!

"Ready?" I murmured.

She gave me a thumbs up.

"Ready!" she whispered back.

She could barely see the book but
it didn't stop her getting stuck in. She
began to whisper and wave her hands

about. It looked just like the real thing!

"I'm pretty sure this spell will make those logs they're sitting on burst into flames," she muttered. "Let's see how they like *that*!"

Logs, fire – she did it all right. Unfortunately, it was the logs on the raiders' cooking fire that blazed up, *not* the ones they were sitting on. The only effect of that was the brigands getting their dinner in record time.

She turned the pages, and got ready to try again.

"Right, then, this time I'm putting a sleeping spell on them," whispered Emmeline. "I'll make them sleep for a hundred years. A thousand years. I know I can get this one … You just watch."

We did watch, waiting for the men to start to nod, willing their eyes to close. And they *did* close. But the spell only half worked. One eye per raider drooped shut, so that they were all winking.

"Hey – you trying to be funny?!" snarled one.

"Who do you think you're winking at?!" spat another.

"Do you want a punch in the nose?" snorted a third.

For a few moments I wondered if perhaps they might start fighting

amongst themselves and solve our problem for us, but the spell wore off too fast for that. Grumbling under their breath, the raiders settled down to their meal again.

When I looked at Emmeline, she was already murmuring the words of yet another enchantment. When it was finished, she turned to me and hissed, "This time I didn't hold back. No more being nice. *That* was a summoning spell. Any minute now, this clearing is going to be swarming with ferocious wild wolves and bears, and they're going to tear those raiders to pieces before you can say 'Grrr'. Any minute now!"

When we heard the rustling, we looked at each other in wild delight. I thought, *She's really done it!* And wild animals *did* appear. Just not exactly the animals she'd had in mind …

I've never seen squirrels look so confused. Luckily for them, the spell wore off before they actually got to the attacking part. Most of the raiders didn't even notice them, though one yelped, "Aggg – a rat!" and jumped several feet into the air before pretending he was just practising fight moves.

Defeated, we crawled away.

"It didn't work!" Emmeline
whimpered when we got back to the
colts, waiting at the forest's edge. "Not a
single spell! Magic *wasn't* the one special
thing, but what else *can* be?! There's
nothing I know about that's any good!"

Piddler came up to give Emmeline's
hair a nibble. I tried to shoo him away,
thinking she might not feel like being

chewed on just then, but only succeeded in startling him, and he reacted in the way startled colts do – especially ones called Piddler. He piddled nervously – I only just got my foot out of the way in time. I still had that foot in midair when the idea struck.

"There's one thing we haven't tried," I said quietly. "One thing that *I* know about, better than anything else."

Emmeline looked puzzled. "I don't understand. What do you know better than anything else?"

I leaned over and whispered one word.

"Muck."

For a moment she looked as if she thought I'd gone crazy, or was suddenly being randomly rude – and then you could see it all come clear in her mind.

"Genius!" she said.

Let me explain. With any animal or pet that lives with people, the first thing you need to do is to house-train it – you need to teach it to not go to the loo indoors. With a flying horse, however, the thing you want to teach it first is not go to the loo *in midair*. There's a word you use to tell them to wait, and another word for when they've landed and it's safe to, um, let go.

That second word would be our special thing!

Chapter Six

Attack!

It was a full moon that night, so everything was weird-looking in black and white. All around us, pairs of eyes glittered strangely, as the colts milled about, catching our excitement.

The raiders would be asleep by now.

It was time.

We mounted and, as one, the troop turned towards the edge of the meadow and began to run …

Over the trees we flew to the clearing. Looking down on the sleeping raiders and their evil cages, I could feel my anger boiling up again and this time,

I let it through. With all my might, I
shouted the word. The colts snorted and
jinked in surprise – they couldn't believe
I really meant it! So I yelled it again,
even louder this time, and Emmeline
joined in. The men below sat up,
bewildered by the noise – and then …

The first few splats
landed harmlessly
on the ground.
"What's
happening?" yelled
one raider.

"Is it starting to rain?" shouted another.

"What's that smell?!" wailed a third.

Then the colts

started to get lucky.

"Aagghhh – something horrible just landed on my head!!"

"Yuck – wet – squishy – HELP!!"

"This rain doesn't smell right!"

The colts were really getting into it now, making every pass across the clearing

count. Neighing shrilly in excitement, they swooped back and forth, bombing the raiders with first-grade muck and more wet wee than you'd have believed possible. What a nightmare!

The men must have thought things couldn't get worse.

Which is when the cages began to explode.

The adult horses, hearing the cries of the colts, thought their young ones were

in danger and went mad. Screaming,
frantic, they began to kick, and
kick … the wood of the cages shattered
outward in jagged, cutting shards,
spiking anyone within range.

It was chaos – the darkness was full
of unseen enemies, noxious, splatting
bombs, terrible screams, and skewering
sharp wooden things. Prince Franck was
screeching contradictory orders – his
men yelled and swore, wiping our secret
weapon off their heads and slipping in it
as they staggered about.

And then, they all just *cracked*. The
entire raiding party ran off into the
forest in every direction, crashing
through the undergrowth trailing curses
and cries, with a few of the colts in
pursuit, their shrill neighs spurring them
on. Prince Franck's voice howled above

all the rest, wailing over and over, "*It's not fair! It's just not FAIR!*"

It was wonderful!

We landed in the clearing, crowing and laughing in delight, thinking we'd really done it this time. Thinking that the danger was all over.

But it wasn't.

The adult horses didn't know their tormentors were gone. Freed from the terrible cages, they were blindly searching for the raiders, desperate to kick and kill, unable to tell enemy from friend. We were in immediate danger – and so were *they*. Unable to see, without their wings to balance, completely disoriented, there was every chance they might crash into one another or run into a tree or fall and break their legs. I didn't know what to do. I just stood there like a noodle, but not Emmeline.

She began to sing.

She'd said before that singing wasn't useful, but she was absolutely wrong. At that moment, it was the one special thing that could reach through all their red rage and speak to the horses. Speak directly to their hearts.

As she sang, the screaming and plunging gradually slowed until the huge creatures had all come to a halt. Quivering and sweating, they stood still and let us move among them, untying their blindfolds and stroking their necks. The colts helped too, whickering and nuzzling up to their parents, reassuring them they were safe, and that it was all over now.

At last the entire herd had calmed down enough that we were able to

lead them away from the clearing to
the clean grass, cool spring water – and
fresher air! – of the hillside. It would be
time to fly them all home again soon,
but first we let them drink and graze
and roll in the moonlit grass to their
hearts' content.

It was a lovely sight.

"We did it," I said happily to

Emmeline.

"We really did," she agreed with
a smile.

Chapter Seven

The Wizards' House

Back on the steps of the Wizard House,
Sweeper had hung on every word. But,
as the old man came to the end of his
tale, the boy frowned.

"But … how did all that help you become a wizard?" he asked.

"Well, I'll tell you," the wizard said. "The disaster was over. No one ever saw Prince Franck or his horrible henchmen in the mountains again. The King may have had doubts about just how honourable it had been, the way his daughter and his stable boy got round the vow he'd made, but he was so happy to have everyone safe and his beautiful flying horses home again that he kept those thoughts to himself. He was *so* happy, in fact, and grateful, that he declared a holiday for the whole kingdom, extra oats for all the horses, and anything our hearts desired for Emmeline and me. Well, we didn't need to think very long or hard before we knew exactly what we would ask for.

Can you guess?"

"Wizarding lessons!" said the ragged boy with a big grin. "I bet you asked for wizarding lessons!"

The old man laughed. "You're absolutely right! Funny how things work out. If it hadn't been for the vile Prince Franck, I might not be here today, complete with long beard, pointy hat and fancy robes, talking to you."

Suddenly the whole street shook again, and more stinky, purple smoke came billowing out of the wizard's front

door. It was closely followed by a white-haired woman with scorch marks on her robes.

"Phew! That was exciting!" she exclaimed as she rubbed soot onto her nose. "Who's your young friend there, my dear?"

"This is Sweeper," the old man said. "I've been telling him about the old days, when we were young. And, unless I'm mistaken, I think he'd like to be a wizard almost as much as we did, way back then!"

The ragged boy was speechless, but his eyes shone.

The old lady smiled and laughed. "That's grand. But shouldn't you introduce me first?"

"Of course, of course. Sweeper, allow me to introduce my fellow wizard and

my wife – Emmeline. Look, the smoke's
almost cleared. Let's all go in for tea."

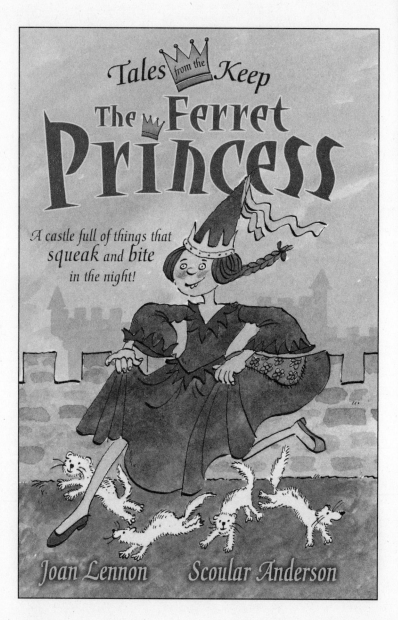

Tales from the Keep

The Ferret Princess

A castle full of things that **squeak** *and* **bite** *in the night!*

Joan Lennon   Scoular Anderson

The Ferret Princess

Princesses come in all shapes and sizes
– from pink and fluffy to ravishing and
regal, and everything else besides.

I'm the ferrety sort. I've got loads more
energy than sense and I just can't help
sticking my nose into things. Or making
a mess out of sheer enthusiasm.

But when two wicked princes arrived
looking for a kingdom to take over
I needed all my ferrety talents to see
them off – not to mention the help of
my very own ferrets!

Tales from the Keep

Wag and the King

Time for an old dog to teach some new tricks!

Joan Lennon   Scoular Anderson

Wag and the King

I'm a dog – an old dog, but a dog at
the court of a King.

My master is an apprentice minstrel.
That's a nice job to have as long as you
can sing in tune, and be nice
about people.

Unfortunately my boy finds not telling
the truth really hard. That could have
got us in real trouble if it wasn't for my
quick thinking and
sensitive nose!

To find out more about Joan Lennon
as well as news about other exciting
Catnip books go to:

www.catnipppublishing.co.uk